Acting Edition

If Pretty Hurts Ugly Must Be a Muhfucka

An Understanding of a West African Folktale

by Tori Sampson

ISAMUEL FRENCHI

FOR PRODUCTION INQUIRIES

UNITED STATES AND CANADA
info@concordtheatricals.com
1-866-979-0447

UNITED KINGDOM AND EUROPE
licensing@concordtheatricals.co.uk
020-7054-7200

Each title is subject to availability from Concord Theatricals Corp.,
depending upon country of performance. Please be aware that *IF
PRETTY HURTS UGLY MUST BE A MUHFUCKA* may not be
licensed by Concord Theatricals Corp. in your territory. Professional
and amateur producers should contact the nearest Concord Theatricals
Corp. office or licensing partner to verify availability.

This work is published by Samuel French, an imprint of Concord Theatricals Corp.

For all inquiries regarding motion picture, television, online/digital and other media rights, please contact Concord Theatricals Corp.

MUSIC AND THIRD-PARTY MATERIALS USE NOTE

Licensees are solely responsible for obtaining formal written permission from copyright owners to use copyrighted music and/or other copyrighted third-party materials (e.g., artworks, logos) in the performance of this play and are strongly cautioned to do so. If no such permission is obtained by the licensee, then the licensee must use only original music and materials that the licensee owns and controls. Licensees are solely responsible and liable for clearances of all third-party copyrighted materials, including without limitation music, and shall indemnify the copyright owners of the play(s) and their licensing agent, Concord Theatricals Corp., against any costs, expenses, losses and liabilities arising from the use of such copyrighted third-party materials by licensees. For music, please contact the appropriate music licensing authority in your territory for the rights to any incidental music.

IMPORTANT BILLING AND CREDIT REQUIREMENTS

If you have obtained performance rights to this title, please refer to your licensing agreement for important billing and credit requirements.

IF PRETTY HURTS UGLY MUST BE A MUHFUCKA was first produced at the 12th Annual Carlotta Festival of New Plays, Yale School of Drama in New Haven, Connecticut on May 5, 2017. The performance was directed by Elizabeth Dinkova, with choreography by Jennifer Harrison Newman, sets by Choul Lee, costumes by Cole McCarty, lights by Erin Earle Fleming, music composition and sound by Frederick Kennedy, projections by Wladimiro A. Woyno R., and dramaturgy by Catherine María Rodríguez. The production stage manager was Bianca A. Hooi. The cast was as follows:

CHORUS	Erron Crawford
AKIM	Shaunette Renée Wilson
MASSASSI	Antoinette Crowe-Legacy
ADAMA	Amandla Jahava
KAYA	Kineta Kunutu
KASIM	Jakeem Powell
MA	Courtney Jamison
DAD	James Udom
VOCALS	Anita Norman
DRUMS	Jocelyn Pleasant

IF PRETTY HURTS UGLY MUST BE A MUHFUCKA was produced by Playwrights Horizons (Tim Sanford, Artistic Director; Leslie Marcus, Managing Director) in New York, New York on February 15, 2019. The performance was directed by Leah C. Gardiner, with choreography by Raja Feather Kelly, sets by Louisa Thompson, costumes by Dede Ayite, lights by Matt Frey, original music and sound design by Ian Scot, and hair and wigs by Cookie Jordan. The production stage manager was Alyssa K. Howard. The cast was as follows:

CHORUS	Rotimi Agbabiaka
AKIM	Níkẹ Uche Kadri
MASSASSI	Antoinette Crowe-Legacy
ADAMA	Mirirai Sithole
KAYA	Phumzile Sitole
KASIM	Leland Fowler
MA	Maechi Aharanwa
DAD	Jason Bowen
THE VOICE OF THE RIVER	Carla R. Stewart

CHARACTERS

CHORUS – Comedian. Ageless.

AKIM – Beautiful girl. Seventeen years life.

MASSASSI – Beautiful girl. Seventeen years life.

ADAMA – Beautiful girl. Seventeen years life.

KAYA – Beautiful girl. Seventeen years life.

KASIM – Confident boy. Seventeen years life.

MA – Refined woman. Lived enough to know.

DAD – Protective man. Lived enough to know.

MIMES – Southern Baptist style mimes embody song to offer transcendence to those who believe. A reflection of what Yahweh sees in us all. (To be inhabited by Dwellers).

NOTES ON WORLD AND LANGUAGE

Believe that you are in a present moment.

Invest in Affreakah-Amirrorikah where everything in this piece is possible.

Places in the text that are ALL CAPS do not indicate the raising of a voice but rather an invitation to explore the degree of emotional weight behind the words.

Ex. Feel free to whisper or sing or invent.

Transitions from scene to scene are an invitation to incorporate live music (a mix of African drums and contemporary American instruments) & (at times) a singer.

This play is to be performed in (one) Nigerian dialect by all players.

NOTES ON CASTING

Grant audiences the gift of basking in beauty beyond Eurocentric measurements.

Akim should not have a lighter skin tone than Massassi. Nobody needs to be tall, skinny, have straight teeth, clear skin, long hair, etc.

BE beauty in all your glory.

NOTE ON MUSIC

Sheet music for the song "Lifted" by Ian Scot Williams, which occurs on page 67, is provided to all licensees for an additional per performance fee. Please contact your licensing representative for further information.

In a world where Viola Davis is not "classically beautiful," First Lady Michelle Obama is compared to an ape, Cosmopolitan Magazine *places Black women as examples of "trends that need to die," where Black Lives Matter assertions fade when Black girls go missing, where Lupita Nyong'o's splendor is regarded as an anomaly... In a world where it feels attacking to others for more than one of us to shine at a time, where the phrase* **Beautiful Black Women** *feels more like a mantra than a fact... In this world where beauty is placed out of our reach...*

Reach,

We

Reach,

We

Reach.

We

THE INTRODUCTION

Scene One

CHORUS. When I say *Funga Alifia,* you respond *Ase, Ase.*
FUNGA ALAFIA.

AUDIENCE.
ASE, ASE!

> *(Repeat call and response 4x.)*

CHORUS. This means I welcome you with my thoughts, with my words and with my heart. There is nothing up my sleeve.

> *(A cellphone falls from* **CHORUS***' sleeve.)*

Well, shall we begin?
We live in a scary world, people.
We really do.
In a time where the collective chooses to *not* appreciate greatness.
The formerly oppressed have become the oppressors.
Everyone's running around rooting for the underdog.
Cheerleading mediocrity.
The hell for?
That's terrifying.
We know the top dog is GRANDER.
Hierarchy makes the world go round, folks
And if given the chance, we'd all covet that number one spot.
That's facts.

*(To begin, **CHORUS** stands center with **MASSASSI**, **ADAMA**, and **KAYA** to the right and **AKIM** to the left. It's a vector scale. They tip back and forth, back and forth. **AKIM** may pose like a beauty ripped from a magazine ad.)*

(The girls do their best to imitate stance, face, shape, etc.)

*(They compete. This is useless. **AKIM**'s scale rises.)*

There can only be one star.
So why you hatin'?

*(**CHORUS** shines a spotlight on **AKIM**. The others fade to the background.)*

*(**CHORUS** aligns itself with **AKIM**.)*

AKIM. Carrying beauty is a *daunting* thing.
Not just pretty or precious,
but REALLY beautiful beauty.
An image so distinct that it outranks all other examples.
You perhaps, may be handsome *except*,
radiant *if*, or gorgeous *for a*...
And how lucky you are to wear your imperfections for others to gaze upon.
Yes. It is such a simple life that ugly people are granted.
All grouped up like that.
I *wish* I had a big nose like you.
Or that awful five head that you have sir, right there.
I'm pointing at you...with the big ass head. Yeah him.
I am surveying around this room at all you ugly people.
So many, everywhere I look!
And boy do I envy you!

CHORUS. Ugly people, do you know how lucky you are? That's not a rhetorical question. I'm collecting data.

AKIM. Funny fact about bone structure, skin, hair, height, eyes, lips, ears, etc.

You can't purchase them.

Well so and so did, but you know what I'm talking about.

Your body is yours. It just comes to you for free!

Isn't that amazing?

A rich person can be born a scare and a poor person a gem. We have no control over any of it.

Let me ask you a question.

When people compliment your looks, do you say thank you?

Why? You did nothing to contribute.

In the same regard you shouldn't feel responsible for your ugliness either.

Beauty is neither your accomplishment nor your failure.

CHORUS. Find something else to be proud of, Muhfuckas!

AKIM. Do you care what my name is or are you too mesmerized by what you see that it just doesn't matter?

Oh, you care? Akim! My name is Akim Chagu. Do you hear that noise? That laughter?

Those are the sounds of the new society girls getting ready for movement lessons.

They get to learn to waltz, foxtrot, jive and samba for the huge coming-of-age ball being thrown in their honor just because they're turning eighteen!

> *(In the shadows, we see the girls performing the dances as* **AKIM** *describes them.)*

I'm turning eighteen too, you know.

But my parents won't let me take part in the society.

Dad just says, "No!"

Mommy says I need to let others have the spotlight.

I told them, "Just let me go and I'll try to be as dirty, disgusting, horrid-looking as ever."

As if that were possible.

And, you know, I suffer every day for it!

So, here I am.

In the house as always, practicing my music.

I love the sound of the Djembe.

> *(Djembe sounds.)*

Everyone says I'd be a majorette leading the band on the field but I'd want to be a part of the line. Or do both.

Someone like me has options.

> **(AKIM** *plays a cadence on multiple drums.)*

MA. Akim?

CHORUS. *(Aside.)* That's her mother.
Notice her high cheek bones and smooth skin.

AKIM. Yes.

MA. Did you oil your hair?
Twist it?

AKIM. Yes.

MA. Rinse your teeth with coco water?

AKIM. Uh-huh.

MA. What about your face?
Did you exfoliate?

AKIM. Maaaaaaa.

MA. Well you don't want to get pimples, do you?

AKIM. I'd love some. Here and here and here and here...

MA. Sarcasm is a gateway attitude
leading straight to full blown pessimism.
You think you're lonely now?
Keep that up and you'll really see because –

AKIM. Cynicism isn't becoming of a woman.
I know.

MA. Yet you continue this behavior.
Why do you look so mean?
That's the trend these days, girls going around frowning
and smacking lips.
Smile.

AKIM. About what?

MA. Tst.
What does that mean, *about what*?
Do you need motivation to put a smile on your face?

AKIM. Kinda.
I can't just plaster one on and keep it there all day for
no reason.

MA. Why not?

AKIM. ...
I'll look stupid.

MA. You will look kind. Feminine.
Want somebody to make you happy and if that's not
happening you're grimacing. Tst. Show some teeth!

(**AKIM** *exaggerates a smile.*)

People would kill to have a smile like yours.

AKIM. It hurts.

MA. Of course it does.
That's how you know you're supposed to be doing it.

Come now, I need you to walk to the store and pick up some rice for dinner. My strong, beautiful girl. Okay?

AKIM. Really?

MA. The *first* store, Akim. You come back here with poison ivy from those bushes and neither of us will hear the end of it from Dad.

(**AKIM** *jumps for joy.*)

AKIM. Got it. Got it. Got it. Gooooot iiiiitttttt. Oh, yeah! Oh, yeeeaaaaahhhhh! I'm going to the store, I'm going to the store!

MA. *(Off of* **AKIM***'s zeal.)* ...
In fact, on second thought, no.
I'll go; you stay here and watch the stove for me.
Not too close though.

AKIM. Mommy, please?!
I'll be careful.

MA. Mommy, please, eh?

AKIM. Mommy, pretty please?
With everything you love on top.

MA. Akim, I don't want to hear his mouth about a single change in you. That means walk in a straight line. Don't run, don't skip, don't hop, jump, roll, crawl, slide, moonwalk, anything. If you see a cracked piece of cement –

AKIM. Walk around it. Got it.

MA. Hurry back and maybe he won't even notice you've gone.
Dad worries about you.
We all worry about you.
This world you don't understand.

AKIM. Why do you assume I don't keep my own set of worries?

MA. Ah ah, go digging for *anything* and you'll definitely find *something*.

Do you have your cellphone, daughter of mine?

(**AKIM** *looks around until she spots* **CHORUS**.)

AKIM. Yes. It's right here.

(**AKIM** *hops, skips, and moonwalks her way to the store*.)

CHORUS. Akim finally gets to leave the house. So she tends to make the best of it. She walks outside and waaaaayyy past the first store. I tell her, "We passed it." She gives me the look.

I whistle.

(**MASSASSI** *moves forward into the spotlight. It eludes her. She chases it down.* **CHORUS** *dims the light, disappears*.)

MASSASSI. Thick. *Southern thick.*

Something to hold on to.

Much junk in the trunk.

Body.

That's what I'm going to call you, BODY.

That little girl sure does have a shape to her.

"Why can't I look like the other children my age?"

I'd ask whoever was listening inside my head.

Afraid to inquire outside of myself.

It was much easier to pretend I didn't understand what all of this meant. "I'm just a kid!" I'd scream into my pillow every morning after I'd completed my nightly ritual

of balling my fists tightly, winding my arms,

using all the strength of a determined seven-year-old to deliver mighty punches to my backside.

Over and over, I'd strike the meaty cushions attached to my back, hoping to flatten them to death.

Make them disappear.

Morning come, I'd run to the mirror to see if it was gone by pulling my Princess Jasmine nightgown up inch by inch.

The anticipation was the best and worst part.

Maybe. Just maybe, today I'd beaten the woman out.

And only the child of me would remain.

"What's your name, girl? I'mma call you Body, but what is your name?"

"My name is *Massassi*."

"That's a pretty name. I'mma still call you Body."

It turns out the bruises only made it bigger.

And it's cute.

Don't get me wrong, I have the equipment lust is inspired by

and that's flattering.

You know, I used to want to be a ballerina.

Saw Zoe Saldana in a movie and she was so rough around the edges. Her attitude yo, was grimy!

She was like, "I don't need your stupid lil dance company.

You need me! Don't you ever get it twisted!"

And they'd be ready to kick her out, too!

But then she'd dance.

(**AKIM** *moves. It's mesmerizing.*)

She was so graceful and it was like her body curved the melodies in the music.

The rhythm following *her* lead.

Those ballet hotshots couldn't deny that she was special.

I'd rewind the film until I mastered all her routines.

Once,

I made the mistake of telling my auntie that I wanted to be a dancer.

She said to my mother, "You need to watch Massassi. With her fast-ass. Talking about she wants to dance. That girl is one step away from the stripper pole. All that body and she knows how to use it."

Massassi is a pretty name. That's what everyone says. I'm like, okay, what about *me*?

Scene Two

(On the way to the store.)

ADAMA. TST!

KAYA. EH-EHN!

MASSASSI. AYE!

ADAMA. Look at her.

KAYA. Thinking she's cute.

MASSASSI. *More* than that. Akim doesn't have one thing strange about her.

KAYA. Her breath probably smells so bad.

ADAMA. Not even. Once, when we were really young, she spent the night at my house. It's like she breathes out Febreeze! No lie.

MASSASSI. I believe it.

KAYA. She's about to walk over here.

ADAMA. Damn. I'm all sweaty from rehearsal.
Eh, my hair is a mess.

MASSASSI. How do I look?

KAYA. Desperate. I can't stand her.

(AKIM *approaches.*)

Hey, girl!

AKIM. Hi! You guys coming back from society?

ADAMA. That's why we look all undone. Excuse us.

AKIM. You're excused.

CHORUS. *(Aside.)* She's lyin'.

KAYA. *(To* MASSASSI *and* ADAMA.*)* She's lyin'.

AKIM. I'm trying.

MASSASSI. You should hang out sometimes. It's like you don't like being around. Us.

AKIM. But I do.

KAYA. Prove it.
We are going to the skating ranch tonight. Want to join?

AKIM. I can't.
You know how my dad is.

KAYA. Strict like a

ADAMA. Warden

MASSASSI. Clank! Clank!

CHORUS. *(Aside.)* Akim's daddy doesn't play.

MASSASSI. What about the school musical? You coming?

AKIM. On a Saturday night? I don't think I'll be allowed.

ADAMA. It's a function. At school. With supervision. It's not like a kickback or anything. Tell your dad you want to see your friends do their thing on stage.

AKIM. I've pleaded until my voice sailed away.
Believe me, he's not trying to hear that.

KAYA. Guess you definitely won't be coming to the party then?

AKIM. What party?

ADAMA. Festival of –

(MASSASSI quiets ADAMA.)

MASSASSI. We come from good families too, you know?
We're upper society girls not countryside bumpkins.

AKIM. I never said –

ADAMA. But you treat us like we're contagious.

KAYA. She's not afraid of us rubbing off on her. Akim's scared if people see her too closely then we'll notice that she's flawed like the rest of us.

AKIM. ...Actually, I'd like that very much. Maybe you can discover a flaw, I've tried but to no avail.

(AKIM opens her body for inspection.)

MASSASSI. Nothing?

(The girls inspect her.)

(AKIM racks her brain to come up with something. The girls wait in anticipation.)

CHORUS. *(Aside.)* This is when a courteous lie would be appropriate.
The brand of false humility that deceives your fans into trusting that you believe
you are just like them.
Even though you are so
much
better.

C'mon, Akim. You got to think quick on your feet. Your feet! Say something about dem feet! Say they're flat and long. Say your middle toes are longer than your big one. Say you have fungus growing between them. Say something!

AKIM. My

CHORUS. Yupp.

AKIM. Posture

(The girls lean in.)

CHORUS. Scoliosis! Good one.

AKIM. could be, ah, a bit, like, weak –

CHORUS. Abort! Abort!

AKIM. It's sort of
toooooooooo straight.

> *(The girls throw their hands up in frustration.)*

Okay, so what?! I'm a perfectly symmetrical work of art.
You know that, I know that. Accept it and move on.
Or don't but it's probably not gonna change anything.
So really, what's the point?

MASSASSI. She's not even insulting us and yet I've never been more offended.

AKIM. It's just, you know, only as big a deal as you make it. That's all I'm saying.

ADAMA. Most people refrain from verbalizing these narcissistic thoughts. It's called tact.

AKIM. Here's the thing. *Most people* can't honestly say them. Anyway, you all are the ones who brought it up. I'm choosing to not belittle you with coyness.
Seriously, who wins there?

KAYA. Is it wrong that I think I'd rather be belittled?

MASSASSI. What a Good Samaritan you are. I mean. Just. Wow.

> *(They begin to walk off. **AKIM** shouts out to them.)*

AKIM. Sarcasm is a gateway –

CHORUS. NOPE! You've said enough. Time to go.

AKIM. Uh-huh,
eyup.
I sensed that.

Scene Three

CHORUS. *(Aside.)* Akim carries these two heavy bags of rice home.

Her arms hurt something serious which would not be the case if she'd walked to the store around the corner.

The first one, like her mother told her to.

Every few steps, Akim stops, drops the bags to the ground and wiggles her sore arms.

She turns her head to look at me.

I turn my head to look behind me.

AKIM. Hey, cellphone dude, can you help?

CHORUS. With navigation? Time? Weather app?

AKIM. With these?

CHORUS. You know better than that.

Akim, you've got a hard head.

Next time the girls ask you, tell them that.

> *(*KASIM* enters.)*

KASIM. I thought *you* were supposed to be strong.

CHORUS. Aww, Kasim, "the boy who sees." Sometimes the past and GLIMMERS of the future.

AKIM. *(Dryly.)* Oh, hey, Kasim.

KASIM. Akim the beautiful is showing her face to the world.

The heavens must be expanding.

AKIM. A few yesterdays ago you should've visioned all of this. That's what they say about *you.*

That your eyes see miles ahead.

KASIM. My gift is true.

But even so I wouldn't believe our meet-cute to be more than wishful visions. Can my senses possibly deceive me in this moment?

AKIM. I see you everyday in class.

KASIM. You see me?

AKIM. My eyes work. Not like yours but they do work.

KASIM. On me?

AKIM. On everybody. I see more than you think.

KASIM. But specifically, me? You see Kasim with those night black eyes?

AKIM. I see you Kasim.
AND Kaya AND Adama AND Massassi and –

KASIM. Nah nah nah. That's too blurry.
Focus, focus, focus...
On Kasim.

AKIM. Tst.
I have to get home.

KASIM. Before you turn into a hood rat? Hurry, it's almost twelve.

AKIM. Your humor lacks humor.

      *(**KASIM** tries again.)*

KASIM. Let me carry those.

AKIM. NO. I got it.

      *(**AKIM** reaches for the bags, throws them over each shoulder and begins to wobble down the street.)*

CHORUS. What a pitiful sight.

KASIM. Alright there?
Looks a bit heavy.
You are leaning to the east. You are leaning very, very west –

AKIM. I'm good.

> *(She wobbles a few more steps before tipping over.* **KASIM** *runs to catch her before she hits the ground. He pulls her up, steps back and allows her to continue.* **AKIM** *stares him down.)*

Don't laugh.

KASIM. I'm not.

AKIM. Don't start.

KASIM. I won't.
  Those are capable arms.

AKIM. This you trust?

KASIM. Absolutely.

AKIM. Steel. Some might say.

KASIM. Kasim
  may be the very one to say it.

> *(***AKIM** *flexes her arms.)*

AKIM. Well. Go on.

> *(***KASIM** *to the world...)*

KASIM. Eh, Akim, do you know her? The mighty in strength! The Trojan girl. The weight of the world she can bear all. Alone.
  Yeah?

AKIM. Yes.

KASIM. Hold on, I'm beginning to feel a vision of you.

> *(***KASIM** *looks to the sky, reads it.)*

Oh, no, oh no, oh no!

AKIM. What's wrong? What am I doing?

KASIM. Akim, you are falling! Ouch! Very hard!

AKIM. Falling?! I cannot get bruised or scratched or –
Are you seeing clearly?

KASIM. Crystal.
Akim Chagu in the future you will fall VERY hard

...

for Kasim.

AKIM. AYE! You are cruel.

> (**AKIM** *looks at the bags on the ground. She
> looks at her arms. Back at the bags. A glance
> at* **KASIM**...)

Not even a giggle.

> (*Before she mightily attempts to retrieve the
> rice. It's really heavy.*)

Fine, you can help.

> (**KASIM** *grabs the bags, throws them over his
> shoulder with ease. They walk together in
> silence before* **KASIM** *bursts out laughing.*)

Liar.

> (**AKIM** *and* **KASIM** *exit.* **KAYA** *moves to enter,
> like someone who's not used to minding her
> personal business. Before exiting* **CHORUS**
> *lights her. But not too bright.*)

KAYA. Ooooooo, you see that? Of course you did.
Genuinely I just wanted to ensure that you saw ME
seeing that.
I dwell here too, *by the way.*
If circumstances had been altered it'd be *my* story you'd
witness on this fine day.

A story of a multifaceted person, FULL of mystery, complicated thoughts and contradictory actions. Because why not?

Given adequate time you'd get to experience my layers.

Maybe next year, right?

Anyway, I'm Kaya and I'm brilliant.

The smart one, they call me, and rightfully so, if I do say so myself. BECAUSE I WILL SAY SO MYSELF.

(**KAYA** *moves.*)

This guy in my trigonometry class approached me,

I'm serious, just walked up to me and said:

"You're not the type of girl that immediately catches a guy's eye.

But once you open your mouth...start speaking, you become very attractive. So never be the silent type."

Then he winked like he'd handed me the missing piece to my puzzle. MY puzzle. Me.

The gumption to say such a thing.

Or was it courage he owned? Courage enough to rescue me from what he deemed my apparent confusion.

(Matter-of-factly.) People rescue what they pity.

Check it, it's not like I didn't know this about myself. Being drop dead gorgeous was never in the cards for me.

Not ugly but I'm not beautiful in the traditional sense – *Whatever that's supposed to mean.*

(**KAYA** *moves.*)

Wait. Stop that.

With the deep breath and the long sigh that you just completed. Stop yourself before you go on this whole voyage about a young girl self-loathing her way to mental destruction. That's not me.

Kaya is not that girl, okay?

I'm just truthful, that's all.

A SOLID SIX.

Seven, when I get to show off these legs. Watch out now!

Assets.

Locate yours and WORK them honey. As-sets.

That's why I'm frustrated that this guy's words. They shouldn't have affected me. But they did because I could tell he believed he was assisting me in discovering my *central feminine weapon.*

Bruh, I don't need your help.

Like I was taking too long or something.

Was I taking too long?

    (**KAYA** *moves.*)

Time. I analyze time and how I spend mine. Given the opportunity to manipulate anything and I'd elect instance.

Instance, in my definition, is the command one takes in time.

It's within this space that we impress ourselves on other people.

    (**KAYA** *slowly spins.*)

Deductive reasoning.

If I slow time down, people would be able to take in all of me.

An EIGHT.

Not that many people do,

But,

TAKE the time to discover ALL of me

and I'm an eight.

Scene Four

MASSASSI. What do you mean she was with Kasim?
Like with him?
Or *with-with* him?

KAYA. I'm not about to play this game with you, Massassi.
You heard me. Go on, fast forward to getting mad so
we can plan how to seek revenge on Akim.

ADAMA. Revenge? What exactly has Akim done?

KAYA. Everyone knows Kasim is chosen for Massassi.

MASSASSI. A stone would reveal the same point.
And that girl

KAYA. Knows that your reputation

ADAMA. And pride

MASSASSI. Will be discolored

(**ADAMA** *begins to sneak off.*)

Adama, where do you think you are going?

ADAMA. Just stretching my legs.

(*With* **MASSASSI**'s *encouragement,* **ADAMA**
reluctantly returns.)

MASSASSI. Kasim is supposed to be my escort for society.
If he dumps me for Akim, I'll be

ADAMA. Pitiful.

KAYA. A laughing stock.

MASSASSI. Or worse.

(*A moment of recognition.*)

MASSASSI, KAYA & ADAMA. A trending topic!

KAYA. HASHTAG: ThrowbackThursday.

HASHTAG: TheBoyIsMine
HASHTAG: Brandy vs. Monica

MASSASSI. I can't compete with the beautiful Akim!
Oh, God...
I'm Monica!

ADAMA. Daaauuummm.

KAYA. We have to find a way to make her ugly.
'Cause for real, that's the only way Kasim will chill.

MASSASSI. Oh! Let's pour Nair in her shampoo! All her
hair will fall out.

ADAMA. She'll just end up looking like a better version of
Lupita
Nyong'o.
Next.

KAYA. What if we set fire to her face in chemistry class?

ADAMA. Everyone will know we set the fire when we're the
ones fanning the flames. It has to be something that
strips her bare but can't be traced back to us.

MASSASSI. Voodoo?

ADAMA. Are you good enough to lay a trick the right way?
Mess around and we're all going to be giving birth to
giant frogs with pigs feet!

KAYA. Got it! The river.

ADAMA. What?

KAYA. RIV-ER

MASSASSI. Girl, we hear you. This isn't a movie where you
say one word and we instinctively know what you're
talking about. We need details.

ADAMA. I'm saying. Can a sistah buy a phrase?

MASSASSI. run-on sentence

ADAMA. Paragraph

MASSASSI. synopsis

ADAMA. something!

KAYA. Look at all these ear hustlers around here.
Do the stretch and I'll explain.

> *(They all "stretch," move in closer and*
> **KAYA** *whispers something dealing with the*
> *RI-VER.)*

Scene Five

CHORUS. *(Aside.)* Here he comes. The boy who sees. Approaching the Chagu home. Like he has no clue. He knows though. He knows but doesn't care. He's stupid.

KASIM. Akim! Akim!

AKIM. Boy, are you crazy? Yelling in the road like that. My dad is home!

KASIM. Have any bags to carry today?

AKIM. What?

KASIM. Bags, bricks, concrete, plaster, cardboard, paper, air...anything you need help with?

AKIM. Ssshhhhh. Please don't speak so loudly. I'll get in trouble for walking with you.

KASIM. I want to walk with you again. Until my legs break. Come outside.

AKIM. I can't.

KASIM. Hold on; let me ask your dad myself. Show him I'm a MAN.

AKIM. STOP! PLEASE. Don't do that. Please don't be a MAN.
He'll see you once and make sure he never does again.

KASIM. Maybe you'll both like this.
EMINADO! EMINADO!*

AKIM. Your voice. What is that?

KASIM. Meaning you are my good luck charm.

---

* A license to produce *If Pretty Hurts Ugly Must Be a Muhfucka* does not include a performance license for "Eminado." The publisher and author suggest that the licensee contact ASCAP or BMI to ascertain the music publisher and contact such music publisher to license or acquire permission for performance of the song. For further information, please see the Music and Third Party Materials Use Note on page iii.

> *(AKIM moves to the thought of that, but she is
> quiet and cautious. KASIM knows. He watches
> but does not touch.)*

I'm your secret. That's fine, for now. Kasim will be your secret.

> *(From somewhere close but not close enough.)*

DAD. Akim! Who are you speaking with?!

AKIM. Myself, only myself.

DAD. Eh-eh.
That means you are bored.
I can fix that. Please, tend to the garden.

AKIM. Come back.

> *(KASIM walks off. ADAMA is pushed on. She
> dodges the light until it traps her.)*

ADAMA. That's dramatic.

> *(CHORUS dims the light. Exits.)*

First Mistake? Opening my mouth and saying,
"Hello, my name is Adama. Nice to meet you."
Pleasantries... All down hill from there.
Lesson?
Be unknown. Not mysterious. Mystery draws attention.
You'll end up like me. Standing in front of a room full
of people explaining YOU.
Yay! What joy! Well, guess what?
You all are going to be disappointed with me.
Believe me when I tell you I have no story to spread.
No troubles to lie. No bones to pick.
I'm. Easy. Breezy.
Cool with the way things are.
What comes, so be it. That's my philosophy.

All this *let's take on the system and change it* is not me.
I'm not built for the *revolution*.
Or the *struggle*.
Or the *people*.
Or the
Anything, really.
Nothing that forces me to be more than quiet Adama.
Wouldn't that be nice?
If my back were *my* back?
It carried me.
Not you or the world or the past or the future.
But no,
I have to be down for something.
Stand for something.
Care about something.
BIG.
Bigger than myself.
When I just want to live. Not feel so connected, ya know?
I want to feel
like an escaped piece to an intricate puzzle.
Just loose. Free.
Easy.
Breezy.

    (**ADAMA** *moves...a bit.*)

My interior is in constant conflict with my exterior.
My body says something to the world that I don't agree with.
It's like...
How can I explain this?
It's like people see me and they assume I carry things.
Trauma.
Pain.

Distrust.

Baggage.

Anger.

That's not in me.

Try saying that over and over and over and over and
over and over and

It never works.

I say pineapples you hear blood oranges.

So I'm trapped in this narrative

Playing my part

With these girls

Who, by the way, are nothing like me.

However,

I'm not complaining.

Don't go saying I got loud about anything.

I don't care about that stuff.

Remember?

Like the wind,

Easy.

Breezy.

(**ADAMA** *moves.*)

Scene Six

CHORUS. Akim in the garden.

MASSASSI, ADAMA, & KAYA. Hey, Akim. Whatchu doing?

AKIM. Love you too. I mean,

> *(An awkward gesture accompanies that awkward response.)*

KAYA. Working the land? That's...cool, that's cool.

ADAMA. Seems like a lot for one person. We should lend a hand!

KAYA. Of course!

MASSASSI. Or we can just keep you company while you work.

AKIM. What's this, what's this thing you're doing? It's creepy.

ADAMA. Helping?

AKIM. Uh-huh, what's that about?

MASSASSI. We're trying to be your friends. That's everything. Promise.

CHORUS. *(Aside.)* Well isn't this a shocking turn of events.

AKIM. All that stuff from before?

CHORUS. That's right, question it.

KAYA. Water

MASSASSI. Ah-hem!

KAYA. UNDER the bridge. Unless you don't want –

AKIM. Yes, of course!

ADAMA. GOOD. Then we are friends. Let us help you with your chores.

KAYA. And talk.

> *(The girls, except for* **MASSASSI**, *all tend to the garden.)*

AKIM. How was the musical? I'm sorry to have missed it.

MASSASSI. People enjoyed it. Everyone was there. The Chief, even.

And uh, Kasim was there.

AKIM. I'm glad it was, um, a success.

KAYA. Some time ago, I saw Kasim walking away from here.

What was that about?

AKIM. From here? Where I stay? Like here, here?

KAYA. Yeah.

AKIM. NO...

ADAMA. She said she saw him. Not that she THOUGHT she saw him.

> *(A beat.)*

I saw him too.

AKIM. AND YES. What had happened was he was looking for my brother to play a game of tennis. But he's not here so I was like, 'he's not here.' And he was all, "Word?" and I said, 'Eyup.' and he was all, "Cool. Tell him I stopped by." The end.

> *(**CHORUS** laughs.)*

MASSASSI, ADAMA & KAYA.
   MMMMMMMMMMM-HMMMMMMPH.

Scene Seven

DAD. Who were those girls, Akim? I don't like them. Who are they?

AKIM. My friends. They came to help me because I never get a chance to see them.

DAD. FRIENDS? They're not the kind of people you can be friends with. JEALOUS. All girls are jealous beings. It is in their nature. Except you.

AKIM. They are beautiful, too! Anyone can see for themselves how gorgeous my friends are.

MA. Not striking like you. Average. Cute. But do not use words like gorgeous to describe people less than. First, it's insulting and second, you're playing games with yourself. It scares me when you say things like that. How many times have I told you it's important to *speak* truth so that you can hear *truth.*

DAD. She does not listen.

MA. If you were not my daughter, did not come from my genes, I too would be a danger to you. Your mother, the woman who would die for you, if I were not of this relation, would pray to the gods to take away your beauty in the dark of the night. I would plead to the gods to scoop the sands that made one and sprinkle it over the rest of us.

DAD. Beautiful Akim, do you hear your own mother's words?

AKIM. What good is this gift if I can never use it?

MA. Use it? Ha! You do not use beauty, dear child. You preserve it.

(**AKIM** *drops to her knees.)*

AKIM. God of earth, god of wind, god of fire, god of the Obamas! Please take my beauty away from me! Start with my hips that don't lie. Then my bootylicious butt –

DAD. Stop that!

AKIM. Please don't forget to take ALL the thunder out of my thighs, gods!

DAD. *(Up to the heavens.)* Haha, please pay her no mind. She knows not what she says.

Akim, you stop that now!

MA. Foolish, girl. Get off the floor. You say that stuff when there is a full moon on a cold summer's afternoon after a squirrel has eaten a tiger and you will get exactly what you ask for. MARK MY WORDS.

AKIM. I need friends.

MA. You need water. Everything else is a want.

AKIM. Fine. I *want* friends.

DAD. I tell you, she doesn't listen.

MA. Shelves of books, all your technology, your brother, Dad and me.

Not enough for you?

AKIM. Not really.

DAD. EH.

AKIM. To be understood. An accomplishment of a friend, right?

MA. Tst. You begged us for that thing. Saying it connected you to this that and all the others. Now it's not good enough?

Isn't this your friend?

CHORUS. *(Aside.)* She's talking about me.

AKIM. It's a device.

CHORUS. *(Aside.)* I like to think I'm much more than that.

AKIM. ...

    Ughh.

    Never mind. I'm going to bed.

MA. Hold on.

> *(**MA** grabs some salt and tosses it over each of **AKIM**'s shoulders and points to the ground. **AKIM** spits and claps her hands over the length of her body. She spins counterclockwise.)*

Next time you'll think twice about tempting the gods.

> *(**MA** and **DAD** exit. A defeated **AKIM** wallows.)*

Scene Eight

CHORUS. *(Aside.)* Someplace where there are trees and privacy.

AKIM. Tighter.

KASIM. Like this?

AKIM. Yeah, but tighter.

KASIM. I don't want to hurt you.

AKIM. You won't. It just. It feels like I'm melting into you, but I'm not seeping

KASIM. out?

AKIM. Or over

KASIM. Just

AKIM. Melting into you. And it feels like peace. It feels like stay.

KASIM. All that from a hug?

AKIM. It's JUST what I need, so tighter, please. And breathe.

    (Breathe, breathe, breathe (x3).)

KASIM. There is a party;
    A three-day celebration of the season of yams.

AKIM. You already know the answer.

KASIM. Not a freak and grind party. A block party. All families will be there.

AKIM. Except for me. There is no way.

KASIM. I need you to find one.

AKIM. Kasim.

KASIM. Look at us. Standing in the forest, chest to chest like a *Lost* episode of *Survivor*.

AKIM. Secret? You said it was fine. You being my secret.

KASIM. Secrets, secrets are no fun unless you tell everyone –

AKIM. who needs to know.

KASIM. That's not how the song goes.

AKIM. Tighter.

KASIM. Will you

AKIM. Squeeze.

KASIM. find a way?

> (*Their breathing syncs.*)

AKIM. For this. Yes.

> (*Shift.*)

> (**AKIM** *breathes just as heavy.*)

MA. No.
No, parties.

AKIM. I like yams too! And celebrations! And fun!

MA. There are many people and your mother has only two eyes to stare them down with.

AKIM. One day I will walk this world, you know this. Let us together make that day arrive sooner, more practice, yes?

MA. Eh, my lawyer, you make a good argument but you know the rules.

AKIM. Did your mother do this to you? Punish you endless days for being the image she birthed?

MA. Akim there are things –

AKIM. What is the age you were allowed to discover?

MA. Things you need to learn first –

AKIM. Why don't you understand me?

MA. Akim!

    (A beat.)

AKIM. Sorry.

MA. There is more to life than pleasing features, I know.
    More to your being than what meets the eye.
    But the exterior is where it begins. Learn that.
    Learn how to live beautifully, my strong girl, eh.
    In a world that will bend you to its will. Learn to live beyond that.
    Your mother cannot teach you precisely how.

AKIM. Why not?

CHORUS. *(Aside.)* Because as most do, Ma sees the world the way the world sees her.

MA. My eyes take in others' eyes differently than yours.

AKIM. I smile at my reflection in the mirror. Walking past it again to smile brighter. I am pleased by the way my face comes together, but this society turns pretty into a burden.

MA. Akim, there is no fault in loving what is yours. However, there is danger in not recognizing the distress in those who are lacking. I need you to understand this fact.

AKIM. I am suffocating, Mommy. In this figure that everyone wants but it is me. I am every inch of myself and I can tell you it is not enough.
    I require something more than feeling trapped.

MA. In

AKIM. By

MA. Around

AKIM. Is my desperate ask of you. I am begging.

> (**MA** *considers this. She really does.* **AKIM** *can feel the win.*)

MA. Maybe the next celebration, okay?

Scene Nine

(Chagu house.)

CHORUS. *(Aside.)* Massassi is maaaaaaaaad! As. Hell! When she notices the grass stains on her white Chuck Taylors after working on the farm all morning. Her eyes keep rolling but she won't say a word about it.

(To **AKIM.***)* Yo, she mad at you.

AKIM. I can't believe you guys came here this early to help me with my chores. It's only noon and I'm halfway finished.

ADAMA. HALFWAY??? WHAT THE FUCK –

KAYA. There is nothing else to do. I'd eat food from the pigs buckets as clean as I scrubbed them.

AKIM. Wash the walls and floors.

MASSASSI. OF THIS ENTIRE HOUSE?

AKIM. And bring pails of stream water back.

KAYA. What is this?! *ROOTS*???

ADAMA. Why do you need stream water when we can just go buy Fiji or Smart or Voss? This is insane!

AKIM. My mother says it's better for your skin. Please go on, prepare yourselves! I'll want to hear all about it.

ADAMA. You should come with us.

AKIM. Me?

That would never happen.

ADAMA. How awful would we be if we left you here alone, while the entire town is gathered for a celebration? Akim, you are finally going to a party.

AKIM. These chores are supposed to keep me busy for days. My parents have already left for the celebration and I can't go against their decision.

ADAMA. Your friends will make this happen.

MASSASSI. We will all get the *(Rolls eyes.)* stream water and wash the floors and walls. We will all go to the party together, keep Akim away from her parents and sneak back here before they return.

CHORUS. *(Aside.)* Akim stares at her friends in amazement. Look at all they would do just to ensure that she had a good time. How could she deny their efforts or request?

Massassi and Adama carry pails down to the stream, fill them and return several times while Kaya and Akim scrub the walls and floors. Hours pass, it's almost night when they're done.

Scene Ten

CHORUS. *(Aside.)* En route to the party. On the edge of THE RIVER.

AKIM. Through the river? There must be another way. That road awhile back.

ADAMA. It isn't as deep as it looks. Ten feet maybe. Can't you swim?

AKIM. Look at that vicious whirl in the middle. And our clothes will be ruined.

MASSASSI. They will dry before we arrive and we don't have time to go back. Look, I'll go first and you'll see. *(Screams.)* Hello, River! It is I, Massassi!

> (**MASSASSI** *steps into the river and begins to swim across. She makes it to the other side.*)

You see? No worries.

AKIM. What's that sound, when Massassi walked through?

ADAMA. Just the voice of the river receiving our passage. Listen.
River! Adama here!

> (**ADAMA** *crosses the river. The river bellows.*)

KAYA. We've done this a million times.
Trust that your *friend* will keep you safe.
Kaya and Akim here, River! Trying to make it to the other side.

> *(They cross. The River bellows. They journey.)*

CHORUS. *(Aside.)* Do you hear that? The sound of the drums? People laughing?
Sniff the air. The sweet scent of foo-foo is mixing with the scotch bonnet of egusi soup. They. Are. Close.

ADAMA. We are here!

AKIM. All these people, look how wonderfully dressed they are compared to us.

MASSASSI. You didn't bring something extra? To cover those scrubs you have on?

CHORUS. *(Aside.)* The girls begin to wrap themselves in beautiful fabric. Akim is without. But I ask you to observe what difference this makes.

> (MASSASSI, ADAMA, *and* KAYA *pull the wraps from their head, fan them out.)*

AKIM. Oh, you all fancy, huh?
I look bare.
Oh well.
The festival is HERE and SO IS AKIM!
Who'll waste no time of details.

CHORUS. *(Aside.)* Akim shines. She moves over, under, through the beat of the drums. Her hips sway in circles as her arms ask the air to dance and it accepts. She's lifted.

MASSASSI. How does she do that?

KAYA. Defy the plan

ADAMA. All wet with dirt from the river

KAYA. And still.

ADAMA. Still she is –

KAYA. radiant.
How many people will adorn her?
The crowd is already beginning to gather by the dozens.

MASSASSI. Kasim. Bet. Not.

KAYA. He will

MASSASSI. Ignore me?

KAYA. He is

ADAMA. Walking over to Akim

MASSASSI. When I'm standing right here.

KAYA. Kasim does not see you, girl.

MASSASSI. I'M RIGHT HERE! RIGHT HERE! RIGHT HERE!

ADAMA. Okay, Miss 'No More Wire Hangers!' Calm down. People are beginning to stare.

MASSASSI. Get Akim to dirty herself in the River, present herself a hot mess before everyone. People would finally *see*! The plan didn't work the way you said it would! Now, my chest burns *(Panting.)* ALL the boys she can take, but leave Kasim for me! LEAVE KASIM FOR ME. Help me cover my eyes. QUICK. One look at them together and sickness comes over me. THERE IS NO PEACE FOR ANOTHER WOMAN ON EARTH SINCE THE DAY AKIM CHAGU WAS BORN!

KAYA. Massassi is right. We all suffer. Look around you. How many offerings have come this way tonight? No dance, no food, no drink, no smiles, no jewels, no nothing. She takes from us even the simplest pleasures and we are left with nothing.

ADAMA. Let's ask of her to be kind to her friends.
Akim is not EVIL.
She is just BEAUTIFUL.

KAYA. They are the same thing, Adama.
You want us to beg like,
"Oh, please, most stunning Akim, take pity on our average looking faces.
Save some men for us.
Hand over a compliment or two.
Tell the people all the beauty TRUE in your friends so they too will start to believe it. Please, please, pleeeeeeease!"

MASSASSI. You think I'd be willing to exchange my dignity
for a man?

I want both.

ADAMA. Dignity is yours to define.

If Kasim is the one you love, Massassi,

be truthful about what you want most.

KAYA. Grovel for pity?

How ugly then would we feel?

Never.

We must go back to the river NOW,

make Akim face the JuJu empty-handed.

MASSASSI. What are we waiting for?

Let us go find her parents, spread valuable news and
get them to send Akim home.

KAYA. End this nonsense once and for all.

Scene Eleven

(Later, at the party that is still going strong.)

MASSASSI. Hi, Mr. and Mrs. Chagu! How nice to see you here.

DAD. Ladies, it is very late.
Please keep yourselves safe and close to your parents.

MA. They will worry.

MASSASSI. Of course

KAYA. We will.

ADAMA. Right after

KAYA. We thank you so very much

MASSASSI. For letting us chill with Akim at your house.

ADAMA. She's our dearest friend.

MA. Akim speaks very highly of you girls. I'll make sure to give her your greetings.

MASSASSI. I miss her so.
Looked around and thought I saw her. Twice it happened.

KAYA. You too?

MA. Someone who looks like Akim? There is none.

> *(**MA** and **DAD** belt out a hearty, obnoxious laugh.)*

DAD. Ahh, foolish goats!
Akim is too far above for another to reach a resemblance.

KAYA. Eyes sometimes play games on you. You see, right over there. In the distance, that girl...dancing – more like grinding – with a boy. But no. How could –.

MASSASSI. You think?

ADAMA. That girl is TURNT aaalll the way up!

DAD. Blink your eyes and rub them tough because Akim would never disobey –.

> (**DAD** *spots* **AKIM**...*grinding. The party subdues.*)

Scene Twelve

MA. For some dimples and thick lips!

DAD. You choose to cross your parents.

MA. 672 days of labor and you wish to bring more pain to me?

AKIM. I –

MA. And stretch marks. Sooooo many stretch marks.

AKIM. Should I apologize for those?

MA & DAD. Go. Home.

AKIM. But I'm already here.

MA. NOW.

DAD. Your feet are not moving. Why are her feet not moving?

AKIM. Mommy?

DAD. *(Mockingly.)* Mommy, Mommy, Eh, that will not work.

MA. Now you want to smile.

AKIM. This is real joy. I am learning. I am breathing, Mummy.
This is a sincere smile.
That should count for something.

> (**MA** *examines* **AKIM.** *Sees her in a mature light.*)

MA. It weighs more than you think.

AKIM. Then please let me enjoy it.

MA. Let me think on this

DAD. Are you mad?!

MA. *(To* DAD.*)* She made it here unharmed, unscathed.
Perhaps we should reconsider.

Do you not crave more for her?

To skin her knees, to bump her head, to laugh lines into her face.

To live?

She needs experiences.

DAD. Absolutely not!

MA. At times you forget that I grew this being from my flesh. When I have to remind you of this I really must *remind* you. Akim, my growing child, have fun

DAD. NO

MA. Eat

DAD. NOTHING

MA. Celebrate

DAD. I forbid it!

MA. *(To* AKIM.*)* You'll stay one night only.

(*To* DAD.*)* It is done.

> *(The party resumes. Drums get louder. Bodies jerk harder. Laughter bellows deeper.* MA *pulls* DAD *in.)*
>
> *(A choreographed group dance in full celebration!)*
>
> *(Everyone gets swept in the yellow ether.)*
>
> *(Create something that feels large, full.* ADAMA, KAYA, *and* MASSASSI *should enjoy themselves until recognition hits;* AKIM *is also enjoying herself. Use the dance to tell this hilarious story of, "Damn, this girl keeps fuckin' winning!")*

Scene Thirteen

(Day two of party. Morning.)

KAYA. Travel back alone? You've never made this trip before and it can be a bit tricky.

*(**AKIM** smiles through her words.)*

AKIM. My mother made me promise to go back after one night.

If I don't leave now I'm sure my father will carry me home himself.

KAYA. The look on his face was menacing, Akim.

You, on the other hand

ADAMA. Are

MASSASSI. Beaming.

AKIM. Ahhhh! Release, baby! Sweet release and I love it!

Probably won't be allowed out the house for a year but at least I know what I'm missing.

NO MORE DREAMS.

The aroma of hundreds of people sweating around you. I know. Music over laughter over silence over groans colliding with beating hearts and throbbing other things. I KNOW.

That touch, you know, bodies...parts of bodies...? Hot, cold, hot, cold.

Fire then ice then icy fire brewing inside of you, from... touch?

How could that be?

But it is.

MASSASSI. Kasim the blaze?

AKIM. Hot like it.

Soft like snow, wet like rain and hard like hail all wrapped in a man that aims his tongue like thunder! I KNOW!

It was sooooo worth it.

KAYA. Do you see how elated I am for you? Let us walk you back into town. On the way you can tell us all about this new found love!

MASSASSI.   Inquiring minds would like to know immediately.

Come walk with us.

ADAMA. *(Whispering to AKIM.)* Run, girl! Like the wind or Flo-Jo or Aunt Flow.

Just be smarter than Jim Crow.

Go, girl, Go!

AKIM. Adama, relax, and take my hand.

With all my joy I could sprint the entire way!

(Shift.)

CHORUS. *(Aside.)* So here we are. One hundred degrees in the jungle, swatting flies, jumping over snakes and Akim is ignoring me. We keep moving deeper into the abyss. I'm not built to function in this terrain. I'm getting weaker by the second.

KAYA. River JuJu! I am here to feed you!

(KAYA throws food into the river. The whirl slurps it up and KAYA swims through it.)

MASSASSI. Me too, JuJu!

ADAMA. Adama, JuJu!

(MASSASSI and ADAMA throw food and cross.)

AKIM. What is this? Why are you feeding the water?

KAYA. The river JuJu won't let you return the way you came without a proper offering.

AKIM. There was no way of me knowing this. Can I have some of yours?

MASSASSI. SOME OF OURS! Now you wanna ask. Psh! Ask Kasim!

AKIM. You trippin' off that?

MASSASSI. Kasim's gaze always found me until you started looking for him.

AKIM. Well you can't reach ten without passing three first.

KAYA. Oh, no she didn't!

MASSASSI. I won't beg.

AKIM. Since begging would get you the same response as silence, I fully support that decision.

ADAMA. Even now, with you standing empty handed on the other side of the river, it doesn't occur to you that things may not go your way. Fascinating!

AKIM. My head hurts so much trying to attach sense to you girls. If you're not asking me to embellish you with compliments, then you require my pity by bowing out whenever you need a boost in confidence. You don't possess what it takes to command that much attention. Jealous, that's what you are and I can't take it anymore! You drain me!

KAYA. Jealous? Aye! We are not jealous.

AKIM. As you scream to me from across the river!

KAYA. Take it back, Akim. We're deserving!

AKIM. Of what?

ADAMA. Everything you have

AKIM. IS MINE!

I shouldn't be made to feel like I have to share the unsharable.

CHORUS. Akim turns around and just like that, forest trees box her in.

The sky lowers the sun.

(She tries with all her might to tear a path.)

KAYA. Ha! You can't move! You either feed the JuJu or suffer out here from heat and hunger.

AKIM. Get me out of here!

Somebody, anybody! Help!

CHORUS. As a device, I don't work out here...or in this moment.

AKIM. *(Into the river.)* JuJu, please let me go and I'll return with much food everyday if I have to. With you I will bargain, JuJu, please!

Please!

MASSASSI. Cry all you want. The JuJu's rules are unchanging for all travelers no matter what they believe their worth to be. You step one foot in that river and you'll be swallowed like Jonah. Go 'head, tempt the supremacies.

(AKIM weighs her options.)

AKIM. If I let go of Kasim

ADAMA. Yes! See, I told you she would do it.

MASSASSI. No.

ADAMA. You said –

MASSASSI. I hate you.

I can say that with ease, absent of remorse.

This is about so much more.

AKIM. I can't break what I didn't build.

You know that, Massassi.

All of this is out of my hands.

MASSASSI. And somehow placed in mine.

KAYA. So we leave her here?

MASSASSI. Yes.

(The girls begin to walk off. **ADAMA** *returns.)*

ADAMA. *(Whispers.)* Adama, again.

> *(She swims back across and hands* **AKIM**
> *food.)*

AKIM. Thank you! Thank you! Thank you!

KAYA. Traitor! Adama, you Judas!

ADAMA. Walking away from a beating heart is easy in
theory but something I cannot see through.
C'mon, Akim.

> *(They toss the food, watch the JuJu suck*
> *it up and begin to swim across.* **KAYA** *and*
> **MASSASSI** *jump into the river meeting the*
> *other girls halfway.)*

Let us pass.
We can all go home and forget any of this ever
happened.

KAYA. Except Akim will still be more beautiful than the
rest of us, we will never be free from it
and all our efforts would have been for nothing.

ADAMA. She's given her offering.
The JuJu won't deny her passage.
It's ended.

MASSASSI. You make our lives miserable, Akim,
and it's not fair to have to be placed next to perfection
everyday.
If only our lips were shaped like Akim. Our skin liken
to the Chagu girl.
You can't even fathom what it's like and you'll never
have to.

AKIM. I can't.
All this appeal has been more hassle than help.

Let me pass and I'll make it so that you never have to worry again.

I'll cut my face with a razor blade.

Nobody will stand to look at me then.

Strip my eyebrows.

Bleach my skin.

Pull my teeth with a wrench.

Anything. Everything. I promise.

Promise I'll destroy myself.

Just let me go home.

> *(Beat.)*

KAYA. Your word is steel? Strong enough to will you to follow through with your promise?

AKIM. It is.

ADAMA. A solution we all can live with.

MASSASSI. She is unbreakable!

What if she does all of this

and people still see what they want in her?

What if this possession of Akim's runs deeper than ocean floors?

Something SHE can't even destroy?

That's a risk I'm not willing to take.

> *(Four arms grab **AKIM** and force her under water. She fights for another breath. She emerges.)*

> *(They push her down again with force. A loud splash. Bubbles.)*

> *(**ADAMA**'s hands tug at **AKIM** to pull her back up. She emerges. Gasps for air. The four arms push her again. **ADAMA** tugs harder and harder, but proves nothing compared*

to the forces against her. **AKIM** *and* **ADAMA**'s
*resistance turns into submission. They give
into the river. They are drawn to its warmth.
Four hands reach to the sky before they begin
to sink. Sink. Sink. Gone.)*

(Green. Still waters.)

End of Part I

PART II

Scene One

*(*MASSASSI *and* KAYA *run as fast as they can through forest, desert, city, farm. They don't stop until they reach home.)*

Scene Two

(**AKIM** *and* **ADAMA** *spin, twirl, flip, and float to the bottom of the river.*)

(*Live music* introduces the beginning of the river as otherworldly and spiritual. What does "Peace" sound like?*)

---

* A license to produce *If Pretty Hurts Ugly Must Be a Muhfucka* does not include a performance license for any third-party or copyrighted music. Licensees should create an original composition or use music in the public domain. For further information, please see the Music and Third Party Materials Use Note on page iii.

Scene Three

MA. Hours you've been gone searching for Akim. Where is she?

DAD. All the way to the house of the boy and he tells me, "Sir, I have not seen your daughter since yesterday's celebration."

YESTERDAY. He tells me.

MA. He must know something! That is the boy with sight.

DAD. Exactly. That's why I took him with me.

(**DAD** *drags* **KASIM** *into the house.*)

MA. You kidnapped him?

DAD. If he is harboring knowledge, I will harbor him.

MA. My mighty husband!

DAD. A protector. A warrior.

MA. Action man!

KASIM. Pause. I offered to come.

DAD. Quiet! Now speak!

KASIM. So, this is the inside of Akim Chagu's house? This chair is hers?

Or is it this one?

DAD. Worry about the one I'm about to break and put up your as –

MA. Eh, Dad!

DAD. He is one of those kids who, who, hugs the trees and then smokes them.

You are useless.

MA. Aye, this boy!

KASIM. Wait!

I don't just pull life from thin air, there is a process to
my forecasts.

But I know my eyes can be of assistance.

DAD. Then come with me.

(*Shift.*)

KAYA. Have you eaten?

MASSASSI. Sixteen hours have left the day. Of course I
have.

KAYA. They say you lose your appetite, when bad things,
when you are holding something heavy inside of you.

MASSASSI. My feet spring from here to there. And WE
sleep

KAYA. Peacefully

MASSASSI. Akim's existence is a thing of the past.
The elders told you how the Juju River works so we're
good.

KAYA. Weeeellll,
they didn't exactly tell me directly.
But from the vent in my bedroom I could almost hear
every word they spoke from downstairs.

MASSASSI. Kaya.

KAYA. It's just that it was rabbit season, I was wrapped
in a blanket and now I'm thinking maybe they were
speaking of a remedy for quivers.

MASSASSI. They drowned, Kaya.
You're panicking.
Calm yourself.

KAYA. Nothing heavy in you? At all?
What about Adama?

MASSASSI. Silly girl

KAYA. who elected her own death.

MASSASSI. So we agree

KAYA. it was by her very specific hand

MASSASSI. Our friend.

KAYA. But still my stomach –

MASSASSI. A break I need!

One minute you are fine. The next you are ready to lay your body at the altar. Was it not you who said we had to choose innocence in our hearts?

KAYA. That was before Mr. Chagu came around my house. Asking my father if I'd seen Akim. I stood there shaking my head like a mechanical doll.

MASSASSI. He'll come here next!

KAYA. No. I told him to ask Adama. That she was the closest to Akim.

MASSASSI. Tst. She won't be there to answer!

KAYA. Exactly. People will believe that the two are somewhere together. Whatever trouble they've gotten into will not lead back to us.

MASSASSI. Brilliant Kaya!

KAYA. Those *48 Hours* marathons are really coming in handy.

KAYA. Mr. Chagu wasn't alone either. Nope.

Has Kasim walking around with him, looking for Akim. And he –

MASSASSI. Quiet! I don't want to hear anymore about this girl!

Even in her death, she is still the most spoken name in this town. When they find her body...pale, bruised and swollen with water, I hope THAT image is burned in people's minds forever.

Scene Four

(In the Riv-er.)

(**AKIM** and **ADAMA** lay lifeless at the bottom
of the river. Abandon your vision of what the
bottom of a river looks like. Think mystical,
spiritual, colorful, and hypnotizing. Stay on
that road and let it lead you to something
dope.)

(From our live musicians, transcendent
music. Building on the atmosphere of
spiritual peace.)

(Two Southern Baptist style **MIMES** dressed
in purple and gold robes with white masks
and gloves appear. They rejoice and dance
at the sight of **AKIM** and **ADAMA**. The **MIMES**
surround the girls; breathe life back into
their bodies. But they are different now. Less
human.)

(Mermaids? Ghosts? Seahorses? Sand? Ice
sculptures in water? Go for it.)

Scene Five

KASIM. Massassi? Massassi? Ma-ssa-SSI?

MASSASSI. Return my name if you're going to destroy it with negligence.

KASIM. *(Dryly.)* May – ssa – ssi.

MASSASSI. Melts in your ears when you use the proper tongue. Anything else and you are beckoning for someone I do not know.

KASIM. People are disappearing left and right around here. You call out a name and maybe the vessel holding it won't answer back.

Adama, her parents are yelling *her* name. All they hear are echoes.

MASSASSI. Call *me* again.

KASIM. Massassi?

MASSASSI. Yes.

Kasim?

KASIM. Present.

MASSASSI. *We* are both here.

That's always true for me. But you are

KASIM. Young. Still growing into myself.

MASSASSI. That's an excuse?

KASIM. Reason. Just a reason.

MASSASSI. Do you have one of those for everything you do?

KASIM. Massassi Massassi Massassi.

Uhm.

MASSASSI. Do you see your mother in me?

KASIM. Eh, you look nothing alike.

MASSASSI. Listen.
>IN ME, not on me, do you see her or your aunts, sisters, grandmother?
>You look at them and you see worthy women.
>You treat them as such. Me –

KASIM. I enjoy.
>Yeah. But what do you see?
>You are so sexy.

MASSASSI. Clearly.
>Anything else?

KASIM. Cocky.
>What do you see?

MASSASSI. I'm asking you.

KASIM. I compliment you all the time.

MASSASSI. No. You grab my ass

>(MASSASSI *points to her breasts.*)

>and tell THEM nice things.

KASIM. They deserve it!
>Oh, and you make sure everyone knows just how much.
>Flaunting all that body in every direction.
>Good googly-moogly!

>(MASSASSI *is not amused.*)

>(KASIM *melodically mocks** MASSASSI.)

>Pretty on FLEEK!

---

* A license to produce *If Pretty Hurts Ugly Must Be a Muhfucka* does not include a performance license for any songs referenced. The publisher and author suggest that the licensee contact ASCAP or BMI to ascertain the music publisher and contact such music publisher to license or acquire permission for performance of the songs. For further information, please see the Music and Third Party Materials Use Note on page iii.

I woke uh lye dis! Flawless

Ooo, na-na, what's my name? What's my name?

I don't dance now, I make money moves. Aye, Aye!

MASSASSI. Stop it.

I don't sound like that.

KASIM. How do you know you've mastered the art of seduction?

Those cut-off shorts.

Whose long gaze lets you know they are CUT just right? Huh?

And they are. Cut. Just. Right

MASSASSI. Yeah, uh, you've got a bit of drool on your lip. Even so, I look good for myself not for you.

KASIM. *(Teasingly.)* A mantra! You should put it on a t-shirt.

MASSASSI. TST.

KASIM. *(Singing.)*

EMINADO! EMINADO!*

MASSASSI. Good luck charm you rub when you need to feel better.

What does that do for me, eh? Functional me.

My friends are missing and you haven't even asked how that makes me feel?

KASIM. The sky is bright orange.

MASSASSI. Don't start that mess.

KASIM. Eh.

---

* A license to produce *If Pretty Hurts Ugly Must Be a Muhfucka* does not include a performance license for "Eminado." The publisher and author suggest that the licensee contact ASCAP or BMI to ascertain the music publisher and contact such music publisher to license or acquire permission for performance of the song. For further information, please see the Music and Third Party Materials Use Note on page iii.

Shuush! Let me read your stomach.

MASSASSI. My soul is –

KASIM. People can convince their souls how to feel. Stomachs convince the mind. The sky is orange, the tide high, the winds are blowing northeast and your palms and lips are dry.

MASSASSI. What does that mean.

KASIM. First it means you need this Chap Stick. Here. Secondly,

> (KASIM *pushes the atmosphere above his head as far as possible. Then he spreads it with his fingers.*)

It means there is still time.

MASSASSI. For what?

KASIM. Look up. You see the orange has to move to red, then blue and purple and finally grey. The progression of fire. The cool air and tide are slowing it down, giving you time.
Before...

MASSASSI. WHAT?

> (*Silence.*)

> (*He almost reaches for her butt or breasts... knows better.*)

> (*Fuck it.* KASIM *goes in for the kiss.* MASSASSI *pushes him off.*)

Why can't you take me in without –?

> (*She exhales her frustration.*)

Please, stand over there and don't touch me. Just –

KASIM. Mr. Chagu has sent me to you.

If you know anything about Akim's whereabouts –

MASSASSI. LEAVE!

(KASIM looks for the response he never receives.)

KASIM. Massassi, you never bother to know more than what pleases you. The deeper you feel the faster you act.

I beg you to seek entirety.

(Short beat.)

MASSASSI. Do you promise that there will be a fire?

KASIM. Certainly. Songs will burn. Songs you know the melody to.

Your palms told me that much.

MASSASSI. Go on, what else do you see.

(A vision appears for KASIM. A moment of recognition.)

(KASIM looks to MASSASSI with surprised fear.)

KASIM. Hands. I see reaching hands.

Scene Six

(Chagu house.)

DAD. What did the authorities say?

MA. For an alert, seventy-two hours at least.

DAD. And the news never runs coverage on OUR missing girls.

Maybe if they see a photo of Akim that'll change.

MA. Dripping blood everywhere. Your knuckles are cracked open and dripping blood everywhere. Give them here for me to soak in warm water.

DAD. I am banging on the doors of all these people; hoping that they have seen my daughter, know of her whereabouts.

Each one says they have not. She could be lying in a ditch somewhere. Murdered or pillaged.

Or worse.

MA. Stop this right now! She is –. The chances of that happening –.

JUST STOP IT!

DAD. So I bang on these doors harder and harder.

*(**DAD** makes a beat with his hands.)*

The same one Akim plays up in her room. Thinking just maybe, if she's inside one of these houses, she will hear me. Now I'm

asking myself what good that'll do. If she's in there. They've got her. Had her.

MA. I SAID STOP!

DAD. Aye! For what? Hearing it is painful? Deep in my eyes these images are embedded and I see them constantly. You say I'm too protective of Akim. But how can you

pretend not to value everything she holds inside of her?
I won't act like it is unreal...an illusion, no!

MA. How soon we forget our own motivations, eh. That
look of terror on your face is because you prepared her
for nothing, exempted her from everything.

You decided how little she should endure simply
because she is –

DAD. My daughter.

MA. She is your beautiful Akim but she is *my* strong
daughter. Not docile. No fool. Nobody's ornament.
My daughter, no matter where she is right now, is
fighting. I grew her strong. Your negative prophecies
and longwinded speeches are accomplishing nothing.
Put yourself to use. Go out of this house; make the
necessary sacrifices to the powers that be and find
those girls.

Scene Seven

(The river.)

(From our live musicians, transcendent music. Words aren't important. Let's rely on the powerful vibration of the voice to petition.)

(Hands.)

(Richly deep colors splash everywhere.)

(MIMES *methodically strip* **ADAMA** *and* **AKIM** *bare of accessories and wipe their faces clean.)*

(Giving actors will reveal perfect imperfections on their bodies. Let's make this ritualistic.)

(MIMES *place* **ADAMA** *to face* **AKIM.** *Close.)*

(At varying times they shrink, cringe, become embarrassed, grow, display anxiety, hate themselves, admire each other, reach or "reach" for a part of themselves that they LOVE. Caress them. Hold on tight. Smile.)

(MIMES *place masks on* **ADAMA** *and* **AKIM'***s faces and proceed to connect with their souls.)*

(They robe them, glove them and before we know it everyone emerges the exact equal.)

(They move as mimes.)

(Lyrics to be sung live accompanied by music.)

VOICE OF THE RIVER.

DIP ME UNDER
WASH ME ANEW
MAKE ME OVER
THIS IS MY LOVING ME DEBUT
FILL ME UP
OPEN MY CHEST
LIFT MY HEAD
NO TURNING BACK
I'M WALKING IN MY BEST

DIP ME UNDER
WASH ME ANEW
MAKE ME OVER
THIS IS MY LOVING ME DEBUT
FILL ME UP
OPEN MY CHEST
LIFT MY HEAD
NO TURNING BACK
GOTTA WALK IN MY BEST

THIS WORLD AIN'T GON' MAKE IT EASY
SO I'M ASKING YOU TO STRETCH MY LIMBS
CUZ I FEEL LIKE REACHING, REACHING, REACHING
AND MY SOUL IS REACHING, REACHING
AND MY SOUL IS GROWING, IT IS GROWING
OOOOHH
AND MY SOUL, MY SOUL IS LIFTED, LIFTED, IT'S LIFTED

I'M REACHING, I'M REACHING, I'M REACHING
FOR MY BEAUTIFUL
I'M REACHING, I'M REACHING, I'M REACHING
FOR MY BEAUTIFUL

DIP ME UNDER
WASH ME ANEW
THIS IS MY LOVING ME DEBUT
THERE'S NO TURNING BACK
THERE'S BUILDING AND THE BREAKING

THERE'S NO TURNING BACK
THERE'S BUILDING AND THE BREAKING
I'M WALKING, I'M WALKING, I'M WALKING,
IN MY BEST
TOO MANY DAYS
I LET OTHERS DEFINE ME FOR ME
BUT I'M STRIPPED TO MY SPIRIT
AND FINALLY I'M FREE, FREE, FREE
I'M REACHING, I'M REACHING, I'M REACHING, I'M
    REACHING,
I AM TAKING, I AM TAKING, I AM TAKING
I'M TAKING BACK MY BEAUTIFUL
WORK IN ME
NOT ON ME
WORK IN ME
THERE'S BUILDING AND THE BREAKING
I'M REACHING
TAKING IT BACK, TAKING IT BACK, TAKING IT BACK
OOOOOHHHHH
TAKING IT ALL BACK

> *(The music builds, movement builds, emotions build. This is a cleansing. This is renewal.)*

> *(I see vessels. I see colors. I see freedom.)*

Scene Eight

(**DAD** *walks from person to person. Day turns into night.*)

DAD. I am looking for my daughter, Akim. Have you seen her?

My daughter, she is missing.

There are two of them. But they look nothing alike.

Akim, if you saw her you'd remember.

Like Friday. She looks like Friday evening.

Have you seen her?

I don't know the other one's name.

My daughter is the one I'm looking for.

She's the

Special

Akim!

Exquisite.

Akim!

She belongs...

Akim!

CHORUS. *(Aside.)* Is here. To the river Dad Chagu has finally been led. Exhausted, he collapses by the nearest tree. He is full of questions unaware that the answer is five feet away.

(*With all the might the* **CHORUS** *can muster.*) Aye, yo! Over here!

DAD. What is that? Beep beep beep. A familiar sound? Oh! The intelligent device. This is Akim's! This is Akim's! She was here! Tell me where she is now, device.

(**DAD** *pounds at* **CHORUS** *the way we would a frozen piece of handheld tech.*)

CHORUS. Ow! Ow! Gentle now, gentle.

DAD. There must be a code of sorts.

Kids these days and their ridiculous need for privacy.
C'mon.

(**DAD** *picks up* **CHORUS.**)

CHORUS. Aye! Put me down, man! Put me down! I can
walk!

(**CHORUS** *jumps out of* **DAD**'s *arms and
begins to walk.*)

(**CHORUS** *faints.*)

Scene Nine

CHORUS. *(Aside. Sipping from a juice box.)* After gaining a juiced battery and suffering through many failed attempts to access my code I finally cracked, spilling detail after detail.

I tell them how her offer was accepted.

How three against one became two against two.

How, hands to the sky, she sunk into

MA. The JuJu river!!!

DAD. They pushed her under until she could no longer resurface.

MA. But you just said her offering was accepted.

Once it's fed the JuJu will only collect spirits that plead to be taken in. Spirits searching for new beginnings and abrupt endings. Akim sought refuge.

DAD. Akim did not want to leave us! They forced her under!

MA. But it was Akim,

The one,

We raised,

Who chose to stay.

Killing was never

In the other girls' power.

CHORUS. *(Aside.)* He knows this to be truth.

DAD. That is not true!

CHORUS. *(Aside.)* And still can't settle on it.

DAD. Instructions from the Chief are to gather our most prized possessions as an offering to the river. We toss everything in and if the JuJu feels it's an equal trade, he will return Akim to us. Only THREE times will he throw her in the air. If we fail to retrieve her, she will be gone forever.

MA. A bid? An offering.

DAD. Call it what you want.

Akim is coming back to us whether she likes it or not.

MA. And the other girl?

DAD. Her father was given the same task in words. However, in action his is much easier. Toss in a cheap gold necklace and his daughter will launch right out. For Akim we will have to offer much more.

MA. Everything

DAD. And hope that it is enough.

> (**MA** *and* **DAD** *gather "stuff," as much as they can. They rush to the river.*)

Scene Ten

(MASSASSI *and* KAYA.)

MASSASSI. He said, "Songs, to which I know the melody, will burn."
That can only mean one thing.

KAYA. That can literally mean a million things.

MASSASSI. A cremation funeral.

KAYA. Or
a BIG ASS FIRE.

MASSASSI. For Akim and our dear friend Adama. Ashes to ashes and dust to dust. Finally this will be behind us when the wind carries off their sprinkled remains.

KAYA. And Kasim?

MASSASSI. This was never really about him.

KAYA. Scaaaaeeerrrrrtt! Say what say what now?

MASSASSI. For real though...
I don't even want Kasim anymore.
Akim can have him.

KAYA. No.
No she can't!
'Cause she's dead.

MASSASSI. You know what I mean.

KAYA. OH, you better love Kasim like he's never been loved before.
Drink his dirty bath water type love.
I'm talking
Whitley and Dwayne.
Gina and Martin
Whitney and Bobby.

Massassi and Kasim type love.

Love that will make you MURDER.

You've marked yourself and now you want to up and change your mind?

I swear on the nail of my left pinky toe, Massassi you will love Kasim until death.

MASSASSI. Mmmmm.

Nah. I'm good.

KAYA. CRAZY girl!

Myself is all I have to blame for the blood on my hands. Falling for the flighty emotions of someone like you. Tst.

MASSASSI. You fell for nothing besides the aching within yourself to be free of the pressure. The standards. The unrealistic example of what we should reshape ourselves to be. We drowned what was slowly trying to drown us.

Everything isn't about a damn boy, Kaya.

KAYA. You better save that feminist woe is me mess for your TED Talk. Who do you think you're speaking to? Not me.

Talking 'bout pressure.

Girl, I saw your face that day.

I know what this is about.

(**KASIM** *enters.*)

(*Full of irritation.*)

AYE! Speaking of the dirty devil himself.

KASIM. Ya'll got the nerve to be out here. TOGETHER. That's bold.

KAYA. Sounds like you have something more to say.

MASSASSI. Come. Let's go to society.

KASIM. When I said you had time. You knew.
Now everyone will know.

KAYA. Know what?

KASIM. You drowned Akim and Adama in THE RIVER.

MASSASSI. A lie! Who would ever say something so cruel?!
So incorrect!

KAYA. Every moment that passes without them I cry out!
Oh, Adama! Oh, Akim! The pain in my heart!

MASSASSI. Pierces through my chest

KAYA. Like a bolt of raspberry lightening

MASSASSI. Bouncing from its roots in the ground

KAYA. Only to trap itself within. Me.

MASSASSI. US! Banging against the circumference

KAYA. Border

MASSASSI. Margin

KAYA. Of the heart.

KAYA & MASSASSI. *(Weeping.)* Ahhhhhhhhhh!

> (**KAYA** *and* **MASSASSI** *faint.*)

> *(Shift.)*

CHORUS. *(Aside.)* Property by property the river takes all
that the Chagus are willing to provide.

> (**MA** *and* **DAD** *throw valuables into the river.
The river swallows them up.*)

MA. MORE.

> *(They throw more. Wait.* **DAD** *takes his watch
from his wrist, throws it in. Wait.)*

DAD. We are giving and giving and nothing appears in return.

We need to offer more. JuJu knows what she is worth.

MA. Does it know we have nothing left?

CHORUS. *(Aside.)* There is always something more.

MA. I am simple, down to only me.

> *(The river produces deep, large waves that lift* **ADAMA** *above them. Her parents pull her into their embrace.)*

CHORUS. *(Aside.)* That girl Adama shakes water from her body as her feet settle on familiar surroundings. She looks around, unimpressed.

ADAMA. Back here again?! I'd really rather not!

CHORUS. *(Aside.)* She attempts to jump back into the river but her bid has been accepted. So she cries out in pain.

ADAMA. I don't want to be here! I don't want to be here! I REALLY don't want to be here!

> *(Shift.)*

KASIM. Save your histrionics!

> *(The girls don't move.)*

Won't you hear my visions?! They say you should run.

> *(The girls don't move.)*

Your fate doesn't concern you because you think you drowned them. However, I assure you, they are not dead. Akim lives.

MASSASSI. She does not!

KAYA. Massassi!

KASIM. AH HA! Attempted murderers!

KAYA. I've said nothing.

MASSASSI. The JuJu cannot return a life it didn't take!

KAYA. I just wonder why words continue to spill from your mouth.

MASSASSI. That greedy JuJu will hoard Akim forever.
If she is not dead at least she won't return here.
This is a circumstance I can live with.

KASIM. That's not how the JuJu works. Their parents are down at the river right now trying to earn them back.

KAYA. *(Audible noise of fear and frustration.)*

KASIM. So Massassi and Kaya are some straight up haters.
Evil, evil, evil, that's what ya'll are.
Hating on Akim just because she's –

MASSASSI. WHAT?

KAYA. Do not pay him any mind!
We have to leave this place.
Now!
Before it is too late.

MASSASSI. No.
Not until he answers me.

> (**KAYA** *in a panic...*)

KAYA. ANSWER HER!

> (**KASIM** *would rather not.*)

> (**KASIM** *attempts to sprint off.* **KAYA** *blocks him.*)

KASIM. Alright. Alright, Alright.
Akim is...
prettier than you.
Both.

(MASSASSI, KAYA motion to threaten KASIM.)

She's a triple-bacon-burger-dog WITH CHEESE.
And I just want to be the bun that sops her up!

> *(Uh – oh. Something suggests that KASIM has to walk it back.)*

I mean, I'm sure there are things you can do, to you know, catch up. I don't know, I'm just brainstorming, throwing out ideas.

Those, uh, magazines? With the makeover beauty tips may prove helpful. Or! Or, just, just like, take a picture of her and do that...to you!

> *(Shift.)*

DAD. JuJu, you will not keep her! If it is more that you want, I will

give you all that I possess.

> *(DAD grabs MA by the waist and hoists her over the river.)*

MA. Unhand me! My own action would have me touch the waters for my daughter. That is no verdict of yours.

DAD. You and the material we have already thrown in should be close enough, *(On second thought.)* hopefully.

> *(DAD swings his arms back to gain power for the proposing of his wife to the river.)*

> *(Just as DAD is about to toss MA, a wave pushes AKIM to the clouds.)*

There she was! We missed it.

CHORUS. *(Aside.)* ONE.

> *(The river tosses AKIM again. This time, DAD drops MA to free his hands. He's not fast enough.)*

(Aside.) TWO.

(Aside.) The river tosses Akim. Ma steps in front of Dad. Her arms stretch four times their natural length. She pulls Akim from the wave and into her embrace.

You know what they say.

If you want something done right, do it the way a mother would.

> *(Shift.)*

KASIM. Akim is back.

> *(The sky turns red.)*

> (**KAYA**, **MASSASSI**, *and* **KASIM** *look up. A moment.*)

End of Part II

PART III

Scene One

(So much bickering taking place.)

CHORUS. *(Aside, holding court.)* I hope you can hear me over the bickering in the background. It's getting pretty heated on the account of Mr. Chagu preparing a fifteen-foot deep fire pit to roast Massassi and Kaya to their deaths tonight. However, like in any democracy, there are objections from others. Citizens seem to be spilt down the middle, some empathizing with Massassi and Kaya, others feeling the need to protect the beautiful Akim. Mainly, the parents of the girls agree that a punishment should reign on their daughters for their actions. Nevertheless it must be fair.

They say that Akim is one person so to sentence death upon two girls for the life of one is unjust. What about Adama's life, you ask?

KAYA. A martyr she chose to be and a martyr she shall remain.

CHORUS. *(To* **KAYA.***)* Excuse you. Manners much? *(Back to the audience.)* So the Chief agreed with this logic and says that the parents must decide which girl will be tossed in the pit. They have one hour. So while they're off playing *rock, paper, scissors*, Mr. Chagu is still not satisfied.

> (**DAD** *enters with* **AKIM.** *She looks disheveled but also like she's bringing the look in style.*)

DAD. It took two of them to submerge Akim. I demand to burn both! You don't need 20/20 vision to see the difference but I'll beg you to put your glasses on, Chief, so you can lay your eyes upon these two raggle-muffins. Now you are ready to see my Akim.

You tell me if her life is not worth these two and many, many more.

AKIM. I hear this for my entire life. Everyday secluded from the same people you expect to regard me.

DAD. THEY MUST!

ADAMA. You can't possibly be serious.

DAD. You were there young girl! Tell the Chief how these villains –

ADAMA. How is it that you can't see the part you played in all of this? With due respect, Father Chagu, it was you who brought upon all this separation. It was you who used us to exemplify her attributes. You can say now that I was there in the river that day, only when it services your resolve for Akim. Was I not there under any other circumstance? Is my life not worth a trial such as this?

DAD. Absolutely not!

CHORUS. *(Aside.)* That was decisive.

ADAMA. Your willingness to toss me aside and annihilate these girls for the uplifting of Akim is the root of all wickedness.

MASSASSI. You can say that again.

ADAMA. Your willingness to toss me aside and annihilate these girls for the uplifting of Akim is the root of all wickedness. But sincerely I plead to know why, by your calculations, we must be lowered for her rise?

DAD. My ears burn from all your whining. Disregard this secondary conversation, Chief. It is meant as a distraction from important matters at hand.

MA. Eh?

For their actions, these two will forever be plagued.

I posit,

To you all,

That death could be an escape.

Life perhaps

Would offer valuable retribution.

However,

If they are to die let it be with a given reason.

DAD. Attempting to kill Akim is not reason enough?

MA. It was never in their power!

CHORUS. *(Aside.)* It was never in their power!

DAD. Chief, you are the one who is here to place an order to our lives. It is your charge to decipher what should be upheld and valued by your citizens. There must be an ORDER, Chief. There must. And it was established many years ago. Every person in attendance today was born into it, knowing full well the systems. Who are they to revolutionize it? Nobody, that's who. Do your due diligence, Chief.

(A long moment.)

CHORUS. *(Aside.)* "Throw them in!" says the Chief! "Leave them to blister in isolation."

*(**DAD** pushes **MASSASSI** and **KAYA** toward the pit.)*

AKIM. Wait! There is something I feel I need to say.

KAYA. Uhhh! Cue the violins and place daffodils at my memorial. Toss me in now and let me burn! Go on, I'm ready to die if it means I won't be here to suffer through her long come to Jesus speech about how hard it is being beautiful and how we should all learn to coexist, love ourselves and find the beauty within. How we should grasp that we've all got insecurities, some just more visible than others. And how that doesn't make them any less vulnerable. Blah, blah, blah, load of crap. You know, that more money more problems bullshit.

AKIM. As much as I'd like to see Kaya's tongue shrivel to dust and her vocal cords scorched, I don't want their deaths on my hands.

MA. What about your father's hands? Though they've proved not so valuable, he is willing.

AKIM. There has to be another way to settle this. For us all to remain here and be recognized in the manner we each desire.

What we experienced in that river was genuine *transcendence*

and I moved

ADAMA. HEARD

AKIM. FELT

ADAMA. FREE

AKIM. This has to be possible HERE too!

MASSASSI. Don't you patronize us with your ridiculous dream world!

If I walk out of here I promise to plot ways of destroying you for good, Akim Chagu. For what is this construct we live in if there are no measurements? No comparisons?

You NEED us to live – bitterly miserable, constantly loathing, meticulously dissecting – so that you can EXIST in all your GLORY. And in perfect fuckery fashion my attempt to obliterate you plagues me as the deranged, jealous one.

I give up...on this, on you. On trying.

Who, knowing what YOU are, what I represent, would keep wanting to reach? If I can't destroy you, I most certainly am not going to nourish you. There is no light if there is no dark to compare it to. There is no Akim if there is no Massassi.

(**MASSASSI** *leaps into the fiery pit.*)

CHORUS. *(Aside.)* Kaya, Akim, and Adama rush the pit, all catching their balance at its edge.

Kasim is a step behind.

They all reach for what is not there. Melodies burn.

> (**MASSASSI** *screams. We hear it less and less. The sky moves from red to blue to purple to grey.*)

End of Part III

PART IV

(Happens in real time (8-10 minutes). Please don't rush this.)

(A contemporary bedroom.)

Scene One

(A cellphone (next to the bed) alarm goes off.)

(She, panting and sweating, lunges straight up in bed.)

(She focuses on steadying her heartbeat. This takes a while.)

(She gets up, turns on the light; goes off-stage to brush teeth, then returns with toothbrush and washcloth, as she just washed her face. While brushing her teeth, she selects a plethora of clothes from the closet.)

(She exits with the toothbrush.)

(Reenters, she powers through her abdominal/butt exercises. She lotions her body. Applies scented oil.)

(She moves to grab her hair products and goes to work on that head, wrapping/putting on/styling her wig. Done.)

(She reaches for her makeup (primer, concealer, blush, foundation, liner, lashes, shadow, etc.) and begins to beat her face.)

(This takes three minutes.)

(She gets dressed. Checks her walk. Checks her stance. Checks her sitting posture. Nope.)

(She changes clothes. She changes clothes. She smiles.)

(She looks in the mirror again. Adjusts something. She stares right into the glass.)

MASSASSI. *(Actor's natural dialect.)* This is my body. I am my soul. These are my lips. I am my word. This is my skin. I am my action. These are my legs. I am my contribution. This is my smile. I am my laughter. I am my courage. I am my intellect. I am my persistence. I am my uniqueness. I am my definition. I AM pretty. I am gorgeous. I am sexy. I am Beautiful.

I AM BEAUTIFUL. I AM BRILLIANT. I AM FREEDOM. I AM QUEEN.

*(**MASSASSI** is ready to enter society. So she does.)*

(Ase. Ase.)